# THE AMAZING ADVENTURES OF SUPERMAN!

## Creatures from Planet X!

by YALE STEWART

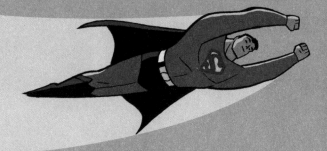

Superman created by Jerry Siegel and Joe Shuster
by special arrangement with the Jerry Siegel family

**PICTURE WINDOW BOOKS**
a capstone imprint

The Amazing Adventures of Superman
is published by Stone Arch Books
a Capstone Imprint
1710 Roe Crest Drive
North Mankato, Minnesota 56003
www.capstonepub.com

Cataloging-in-Publication Data is available at the Library of Congress website.
ISBN: 978-1-4795-5734-9 (library binding)
ISBN: 978-1-4795-5738-7 (paperback)

Summary: When a swarm of unearthly beings strikes Earth, SUPERMAN and GREEN
LANTERN will be fighting for their lives as they take on the . . . Creatures from Planet X!

Editor: Donald Lemke
Designer: Bob Lentz

Printed in the United States of America in Stevens Point, Wisconsin.
032014    008092WZF14

# TABLE OF CONTENTS

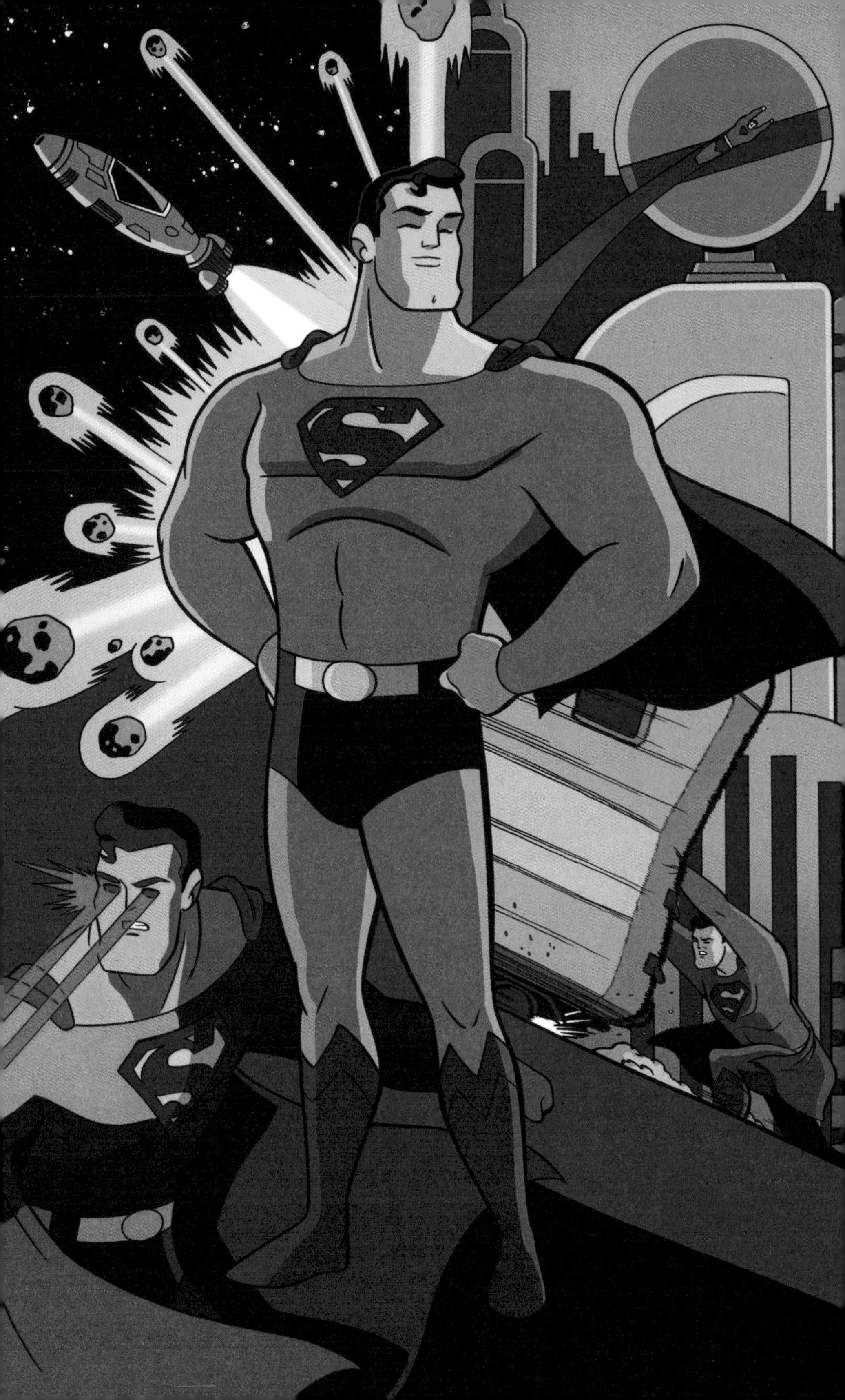

Born among the stars.
Raised on planet Earth.
With incredible powers,
he became the
World's Greatest Super Hero.
These are...

# Chapter 1

# AIR SHOW

Reporter Clark Kent looks

up at the sky. "A perfect day

for an air show," he says.

A dozen jets soar high

above him, performing

tricks. The crowd cheers.

Suddenly, one jet begins

to rock, shake, and smoke.

"What's happening?" says

the pilot, Hal Jordan.

Hal looks outside his jet.

He can't believe his eyes . . .

Hundreds of glowing

yellow insects attack the jet!

They tear apart its wings.

The jet begins to fall.

On the ground, the crowd runs and hides. Clark Kent doesn't move.

"This looks like a job for Superman!" says Clark. He takes off his glasses and shirt. A uniform is beneath.

"I must save that pilot!"

Superman says. **WHOOSH!**

He soars into the sky.

**BOOM!** The jet explodes in

a flash of green light.

"Green Lantern!" says Superman. He greets his super hero friend.

 "The one and only," replies Hal Jordan, wearing his green power ring.

"What planet did these creatures come from?" asks Superman. "I've never seen anything glow that color."

Green Lantern stares at

the yellow insects. "I have."

He tightens his fist. "This is

the work of Sinestro!"

# Chapter 2

# RING OF FEAR

In the city of Metropolis,

Sinestro stands atop the

Daily Planet Building. He

creates thousands of insects

with his yellow ring. "My

plan is working!" he shouts.

Sinestro's insects swarm the streets below. People scream in fear.

"Their fear is giving me power," he says, laughing. "Soon, I'll be strong enough to take over the city!"

The super heroes arrive

at the Daily Planet Building.

"Great plan, Sinestro,"

says Green Lantern.

"But I hope you planned

on us," adds Superman.

With super-speed, the
hero flies at Sinestro. The
villain creates a giant insect
shield with his power ring.
**THUD!** The shield stops
Superman in midair.

"I can't hit him!" says
the Man of Steel.

"His ring is powered by fear," Hal replies. He points his own ring at the shield. "But there's something even more powerful . . ."

# Chapter 3

# TEAMWORK!

"Green Lantern's light!"
Green Lantern shouts.

With his ring, the hero can create anything he can imagine. A jackhammer appears in the sky.

**WHAM! WHAM!**

Green Lantern hammers
at Sinestro's shield. The
glowing, yellow insects
won't crack or chip.

"Time to break out the
big gun!" Hal jokes.

Green Lantern creates a
giant cannon with his ring.
**KA-BLAMO!** He blasts
the shield with cannonballs.

The shield of insects does not break. In fact, it grows twice as large! "Give up!" Sinestro shouts. "Your weapons are useless."

Superman turns to Green Lantern. "Maybe it's not the weapons," says the hero. "Maybe it's the ammo."

Green Lantern smiles. "Get in," he replies.

Superman climbs inside
Green Lantern's cannon. He
straightens out his body like
a missile.

"Ready . . ." he says.

"Aim . . ." adds Hal.

"FIRE!" the heroes shout.
**BOOM!** In a blinding
flash, Superman explodes
from the cannon. He strikes
the shield with his fists.

**CRASSSH!** This time, the shield shatters. The insects crumble into powder and disappear.

"NO!" cries Sinestro.

Green Lantern traps the super-villain inside a cage of green energy.

"One thing is definitely more powerful than fear," says Superman.

"What's that?" asks Hal.

"Teamwork," replies the Man of Steel, waving goodbye to his pal. "Thanks for the amazing adventure!"

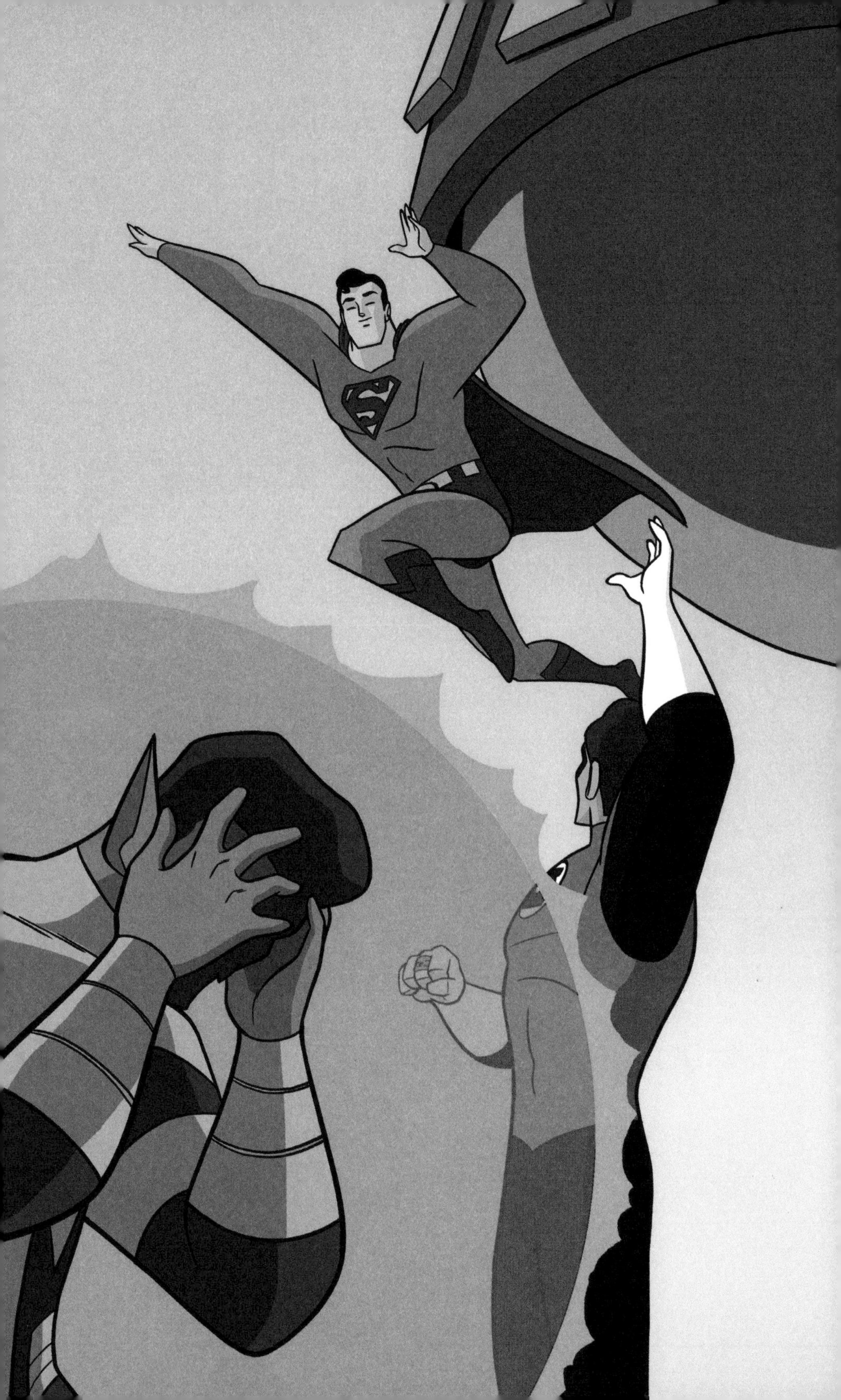

# SUPERMAN'S SECRET MESSAGE!

Hey, kids! What's a super hero's greatest power?

Use the code below to solve the secret message!

| | | | | | | | | | | | | |
|---|---|---|---|---|---|---|---|---|---|---|---|---|
| A | B | C | D | E | F | G | H | I | J | K | L | M |

| | | | | | | | | | | | | |
|---|---|---|---|---|---|---|---|---|---|---|---|---|
| N | O | P | Q | R | S | T | U | V | W | X | Y | Z |

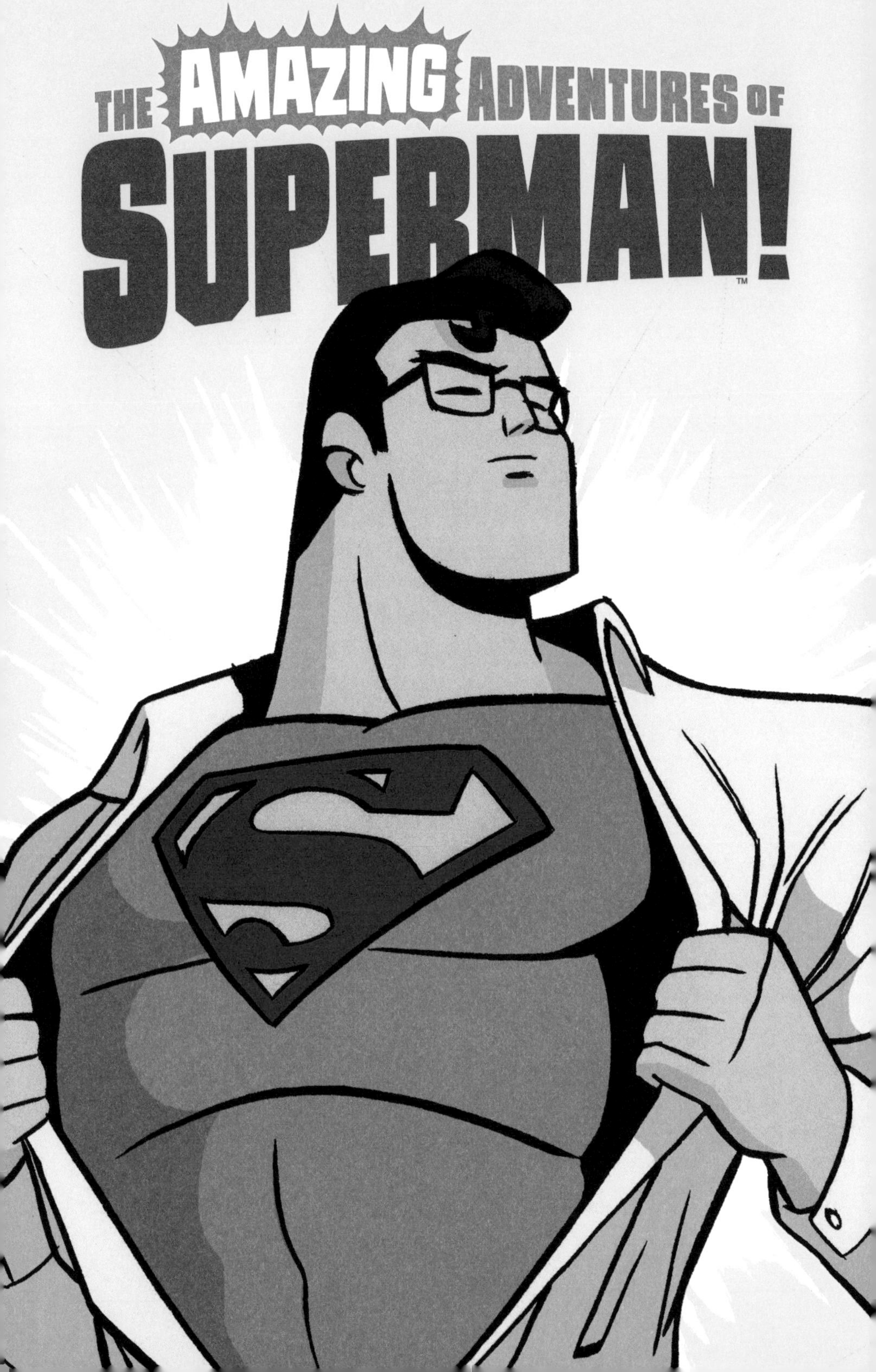
THE AMAZING ADVENTURES OF
SUPERMAN!™

*air show* (AIR SHOH)—an event where pilots show their skills to fly aircraft in unusual and exciting ways

*crumble* (KRUHM-buhl)—to break into small pieces

*imagine* (i-MAJ-uhn)—to picture something in your mind

*jackhammer* (JAK-ham-ur)—a machine used to drill hard materials

*swarm* (SWORM)—a group of insects that gather or move in large numbers

*uniform* (YOO-nuh-form)—a special set of clothes worn by a super hero

*villain* (VIL-uhn)—an evil person